King of Owls

John Stapylton

Contents

Song of the Forest

- -

Your POV:

I release small grunts while trudging through the thick mud coating the forest floor and shoving aside any branches that got in my way. Every now and again my brown boots would sink into the earth, slowing my pace quite a bit, but that didn't bother me much. It's not like I'm in a hurry, and I'm positive this'll be the last place anyone would come looking for me. This dense, gloomy forest is shrouded in mystery and is so very strange. No one knows of it's existence but me, at least that's how it appears.

The place looks as though it's been left untouched by man, which is impossible, right? Especially with how big it is. Surely, one other person would've gotten curious about this place. This is my first time coming inside, though, and, honestly, I feel as though I stepped into another world. It kind of reminds me of my dad, who would always tell me stories when I was younger about enchanted forests and creatures one could only dream about.

It fills me with a sense of nostalgia that calms my dying rage, but I don't concern myself with the enigma that is this forest. It's not important right now. I just need a place where I can disappear from the outside world and not have to worry about anything that's been stressing me out lately. I breathe out a sigh while leaning against a tree for a break, wishing to take off my boots and massage my aching feet. I've been walking for so long, and my legs feel so sore.

While I take a moment to catch my breath, I have a look at my surroundings. Though the overall atmosphere is creepy as all heck, I find the place oddly relaxing. The air is so fresh, and it's peaceful and quiet, save for the twittering birds and buzzing insects. The only thing that really bugs me is the glowing eyes staring down at me from the bare branches twisting overhead. They belong to many different species of owls that have a variety of colors and sizes, but if that wasn't strange enough, their attention only resides on me, and if I walk further into the forest they seem to multiply.

It's like they know I don't belong here. I gulp down my saliva to soothe my dry throat while staring at one that cocks it's head in a quick manner that nearly causes me to flinch. Nervously, I venture deeper into the foggy towers of trees. The bare trees eventually come to an end as I pass more and more that are covered in vibrant green leaves. No new owls appear, though, the ones from before seem to be following close behind.

'What is their deal?' I stop in my tracks upon hearing a faint sound that comes from no natural source and look around. My spine tingles upon hearing the eerie whistle of, what I believe comes from, a flute, or perhaps a similar instrument. Unable to contain my curiosity, I follow after the sad, hypnotic music. The sound was so soft and alluring that I couldn't stop myself, even though I knew it was probably a bad idea. As I get closer to the source, I start to realize the sound is coming from above, so I look up ahead of me and nearly feel my heart stop. Only a few feet away, a peculiar figure dressed in a cloak of brown feathers sits upon the winding branches with their back, thankfully, towards me. I don't think they notice me, yet I can't help but feel a little on edge.

'Who is that, and why are they here? What's with the cloak?' Quickly and quietly, I hide behind the trunk of the nearest tree just to be safe before peeking out at the figure while making sure my form is not visible if they were to turn around. As suspected, a wooden flute is held in the stranger's hands, while they play the melancholy melody with delicate finger movements to block the holes, forming different sounds. I found myself entranced by the being's music and lean my head against the bark of the tree I hide behind.

The music comes to an abrupt stop, and the instrument is set down onto the person's lap. I gasp and cover my entire body behind the tree when I saw they were about to turn around. A few quick breaths escape my mouth, so I cover it in order to block the sound. I hear a crack, and nothing but silence follows. I stand still for awhile, heart racing in fear, before taking the risk of peering around the tree, regardless of the possibility that the person would appear right in front of me, to take another look at the sturdy branch the stranger was perched upon. Key word: was. They had mysteriously vanished into thin air. My brows knit together in confusion, while I look around, but I catch no sight of them.

'Where did they go?' The being's disappearance made me feel a bit uneasy, and it didn't help that the number of birds watching me nearly doubled. I shake my head, deciding to move forward and forget about the unknown flute player. With light steps, I continue my journey to the heart of the forest. I take a moment to appreciate the stillness of my surroundings.

This will be the perfect place to hide away from society. Though, it's still uncomfortable walking around while being stalked by owls. I've never seen so many in my life, well, in person that is. I've seen plenty of owls in the books I've read, and I even recall an urban legend I once heard of about a king of owls. It was one of my father's stories, actually.

It was an old, forgotten tale that's only a distant memory in my head. The only thing I seemed to remember is the king and nothing more, but, again, such things are not important right now. Eventually, I grow tired of traveling, and it's already starting to get dark out, which isn't good. I needed to find shelter and quick incase the thick clouds hanging above decide to send down rain. Besides, who knows what beasts roam this place at night? Luckily, it isn't long before I stumble upon a small cave hidden within the light fog that had blanketed the ground not long after the sun went down.

I take a seat on the dirt floor and tuck my knees to my chest. I don't regret my decision in the slightest. I've read enough about the outdoors and have enough basic survival skills to know what to do out here. The only thing I'm really upset about is that I stormed out without bothering to grab any necessary supplies. I have no food, no water, no extra clothes or even a blanket. I have nothing with me, but the clothes on my back.

I'm determined, though. I'm not going back until I'm ready to face the world again. Until that day, I want to live somewhere where I can be free. Hopefully, this forest is just what I'm looking for. I feel exhaustion overtake me as I lie on my back and stare up at the rocky ceiling with half-lidded eyes. Gradually, they shut, and my breathing slows as I listen to the sounds of the forest. The chirping of crickets and hooting of the owls in the trees lulls me to sleep. It was almost like the forest was singing a lullaby just for me.

However, I was left unaware of the bright, orange eyes that observed me from afar.

Survival of the Fittest

Y/N: Your Name•E/C: Eye Color

Author's POV:

The dead of night burst alive with sounds of hooting owls and noisy crickets, but, regardless of all the commotion, a single figure sleeps soundly in a small cave surrounded by tall trees. A layer of thick fog seeps in through the opening, forming a heavy dampness in the place and causing glistening droplets to form on the female's skin. Soft, near-silent thuds travel along the roof of the natural structure as a curious creature lurks within the darkness lit up only by the quarter moon and twinkling starlight, but even those are partially covered by the dark clouds scattered above. Deciding to peek inside the cave before making an entry, the male stops at the mouth of it before getting on all fours to hang his head and look inside. Chestnut brown locks drape downward before his neck tilts sharply to the point where his ear touches his shoulder when his piercing, orange eyes land on the sleeping figure inside.

Her back faced him, but it's quite obvious she's unconscious due to the very faint snores escaping her parched lips. Very quietly, the figure climbs around the entrance of the cave without ever taking his eyes off the person intruding on his territory. Cautiously, on all fours, the male slinks over to the girl with intrigue, not creating a single sound as he gets closer and closer. His head tilts side to side at odd angles while observing her vulnerable form before stretching an arm towards her face to turn her over. He takes her chin into his hand with light touches and shifts it to fully view her feminine features.

Almost instantly, he pulls away and jumps back a few steps in skittish movements when her eyes twitch beneath the skin of their lids. Not wanting to get caught spying on the stranger, he turns and runs out of the cave before scurrying up the nearest tree to hide amongst its winding branches and deep green leaves. His heart pumps wildly in his chest while he stares down, watching for any movement, but nothing caught his eyes. She didn't wake, and, though he wished to investigate further, he thought it less risky to remain where he is until the sun arose. He was on the brink of nodding off when a shuffle of dirt caught his keen ears, and, immediately, he looked down, watching closely as this human female sits up and stretches her arms above her head. The girl then stands up and pushes at her lower back to relieve any built up tension with a satisfying crack. The sharp sound caused the creature to flinch and rustle some leaves, but the person below didn't seem to notice or care.

'I guess this cave will work as a good base for now,' Y/N thinks to herself before nearly rubbing her eyes with her dirty palm. She pulls her hand away after realizing it's caked with dirt from the floor of her temporary home and carelessly wipes it on her pants. She doesn't waste time on worrying about the possibility of forgetting the cave's location, for the chances of that are slim. Her sense of direction is actually quite good; in fact she can easily find her way back to civilization if she ever decides to return to the life she left behind. At the moment, however, that isn't a part of the agenda, wilderness survival is.

'Okay, what do I need to do?' She wonders while walking out of the rock formation she slept in and looking around. There was nothing notable, just the same tall trees and gloomy atmosphere, which she oddly finds comforting. She was thankful for the absence of spying owls, however, for they were what put her off most on her arrival. Likely, they are all fast asleep now that it's morning, but she wonders if they'll return by the time dusk rolls around.

What she didn't realize, however, was that one is still with her, just well hidden in the trees to avoid being spotted. It was at a time like this, he was proud to be a master of stealth, though, he wished he could get a bit of shut eye. He shook the tiredness from his brain, wishing to remain vigilant while stalking the stranger invading his land. Y/N grabs a stick from the ground before sitting and writing a list in the dirt. There are many things she needs to sort out before night falls.

'Okay, so I'm gonna need a fire. I should start by gathering sticks, then worry about it from there. I'll need food and water too, so those are my top priorities, especially the water.' At the very thought of the refreshing liquid, her tongue felt dry, like her mouth had been stuffed with cotton. She'd most definitely need that sooner rather than later.

Her E/C eyes shut, blocking out any visual distractions as she sits silently and listens for one sound in particular. She heard many things, like the cheerful twittering of birds, the soft whistle of the breeze that blows through her hair and rustles the leaves, and the persistent thumping of a woodpecker chipping away at bark on a nearby maple. Then, there it was. The sound was faint, but easily recognizable as rushing water. She opens her eyes and hops to her feet before walking in the direction she heard it from.

Surprised by her sudden leave, the creature in the trees quickly follows after, being as quiet as a mouse to blend in with his surroundings. During her journey, Y/N would revel in the pleasant silence, completely oblivious to her stalker's curious stare. There is a peace out here that she just couldn't get back home with all the cars that'd drive by on the streets and the noisy conversations people would have with each other. The increase in flying insects and heightened volume of flowing water was enough to tell her that she is almost where she wanted to be, which was great, except for the annoying gnats that seem to enjoy getting in her face. Constantly, she'd swat at the buzzing bastards trying to land on her skin as she trudges through the overgrowth of plants in her way.

Looking down, her eyes grew in shock at the sight of numerous animal tracks in the mud heading in the same direction as her. Clearly, she is on the right track. A smile breaks out on her lips upon coming across a stream of crystal clear water, which is perfect for her situation, and what's greater is that it's not too far from her cave. The girl falls to her knees, almost scared to touch the water, for it was almost like it was never touched by human hands, which she'd honestly believe. She sticks her hands in and smiles at the cool temperature while washing away the dirt on her hands before cupping them together to scoop up the water.

She knows she has no way of filtering it, which can be quite hazardous, even if the water does look clean, so she drank only what was in her hands to hydrate herself. It tasted fine to her, but that meant nothing. There could be lots of harmful bacteria that she doesn't know about swimming in that liquid, but, again, she doesn't have much of a choice. She scoops up some more, but uses this handful to wash the dirt off her face from when she slept. Afterwards, she sits to observe the scenery and takes note of some fish swimming upstream.

'That can be a good food source, but I'll need a weapon or a net of some kind if I'm going to catch anything.' She sighs, knowing this is going to take a lot of hard work, but she's up for it. She wouldn't have come out here if she didn't have some clue of how to survive. Drinking one last handful of water, Y/N stands and walks back towards home base in search of sticks. Small sticks, big sticks, misshapen sticks, it didn't matter to her so long as they'll be useful. Her arms were full after about an hour, and she decided to bring it all back to the cave before setting out for more, only she didn't only grab sticks this time around, but rocks too.

Small, flat rocks were ideal for what she has planned, so she only took those. When she brought it all back, she separated wood into two piles: one for fire, another to sharpen to a point. Taking one of the rocks within her hand, Y/N glides the side of it against one of the stone walls repeatedly at a quick pace, accidentally hurting her fingers from time to time, but the method was working, albeit slowly. All the while, her spectator watches with interest, having no clue as to what the human is doing. After growing tired with the rock, the girl sets it down before deciding to avert her focus back to the water situation. She needs a method of collecting it in a manner that'll be effective, and, if she could think of a way to collect rain water as well, that'd be just swell. This, however, will be a difficult task, since she doesn't have much on her and carrying water in her boots probably isn't the best idea either. Going back and forth everyday when thirsty will eventually get tiring too.

"Baby steps," she mutters to herself, knowing that it'll take time to devise an effective way of going about this. She might not have a solution today or tomorrow, so she'll just have to do the best with what she has. Her gaze lifts to the forest outside her shelter and gives a soft hum in thought.

'Maybe there'll be something out there that'll help?' Getting to her feet, she wanders out again in search of something useful to carry water in. Her search went on for about two hours before she came across a misshapen stone the size of her head. The center of it had worn down over time, forming a shallow bowl, which is quite lucky for the young adult.

'This'll do. It might not fit much, but it's better than nothing.' Satisfied with her find, Y/N finds her way back to the stream for another drink of water before scrubbing the dirt and moss off the semi-heavy rock to the best of her ability. Lastly, she fills the small crater before smiling victoriously when she finds it successfully holds the clear fluid. With a steady hand, the human brings it back to the cave and sets it down someplace safe, where it won't be knocked over. A head tilts from above, having watched the whole spectacle. The man was surprised by her survival knowledge and couldn't wait to find out what she'd do next, and, yet, he still knows to be weary of this intruder. He does not know her well enough to know if she's a threat or not, but one thing's for sure,

She had certainly caught his attention.

Hungry Hunter

Y our POV:

With a tired huff, I finish up sharpening my third rock on the wall of the cave I've sought refuge in and set it aside next to the sticks, which I've also shaped into a deadly point. Only one of the rocks I've sharpened are long enough to form the shape of a knife, while the others had broken and chipped into dull, makeshift blades, but, hopefully, I can still find some use for them. Noting how late it's gotten, I peer out of the cave and find the bright sun descending from the bleak, cloudy sky, which marks the end of my first official day in the wilderness. I pick up a new rock and use it to mark a line on the wall. I'd like to have some understanding of how much time passes of me staying in this forest, so I plan to do this daily.

A fierce growl of hunger sounds from my stomach, which seemingly twists in a painful manner, but I ignore it. I've gone one day without food. I should be fine, but I need to try getting some first thing in the morning. With luck, I'll find some edible berries or plants, or perhaps I'll even manage catching an animal. I highly doubt I'll snare anything my first try, but, hopefully, after some practice, I'll at least be able to spear some fish out of the stream. I give a soft sigh while leaning against the wall.

I'm not feeling very cold, so I don't think I'll bother making a fire tonight or at least this very second; instead I take a moment to relax. My first day had been very tiring, what with all the walking and hauling things back to the cave, but I'm fine. I didn't expect this to be easy. I know I can do this. My eyelids droop, and, at times, would shut as the hooting of owls sound from right outside my dwelling place. Seems they've returned. I don't understand their fascination with me; it's very unsettling, but what am I supposed to do about it?

'Maybe if I throw a rock at them, they'll go away? No, bad idea. They might swarm and attack me. Oh, well. Not like they're doing anything other than watching.' Finally, the exhaustion gets to me, and I begin to nod off.

My head starts lulling to the side as my body slumps against the wall to rest.

————————

The next morning, I wake up with a groan and slowly sit up while rubbing my sore back. The dirt isn't exactly comfortable. Hopefully, I'll manage to find something with a soft hide to lie on, though, I won't get my hopes up. I doubt I'll be able to catch anything big enough to make a difference. A girl can dream, though.

I remove the white, knitted scarf from around my neck and tie it across my body before gabbing my makeshift knife and securing it between the folds of the scarf. I also grab one of the sharpened sticks before heading out in search of food. With silent steps, I trudge the forest floor with my gaze on the muddy ground in search of tracks. Eventually, I happen upon deer tracks, so I follow those while listening to the chirping birds in the trees. I would try for one of those, but it would be too hard to catch a bird. They're much too fast and are small targets.

I'd probably have better chances with a deer. I stop upon reaching a small clearing and standing in the middle of the tall grass is a lovely doe feasting upon the dark green blades. Suddenly, her ears perk and she looks in my direction, so I remain still, even holding my breath as to not startle it. I gulp slightly while staring into her big, black orbs as her nose twitches. It almost felt like she was gazing into my soul.

My lips part in surprise when the deer takes a cautious step towards me, then another and another. I tense slightly, but remain in place as she stops in front of me before stretching her neck a bit to sniff me. Not making any sudden movements, I slowly raise my hand to the doe's face. She doesn't even try to run as I gently pet the fur between her eyes. I breathe out a laugh at how amazing this is, but my lips then shape into a small frown. Sadly, I intend to eat the animal. I walk around the doe as she bends her neck down to eat the grass while reaching for the stone knife in my scarf. I gently pet her shoulders before looking to where I need to aim. I take a deep breath to mentally prepare myself for what I was about to do as I raise the blade.

"I'm sorry," I mutter before thrusting the knife forward, aiming for a vital part. However, before the sharp object could even make contact with the animal, a cloaked figure drops down from one of the trees and pushes me away from the deer hard enough to send me onto my back. My weapon falls from my hand, but before I could reach for it, the stranger stomps on the stone repeatedly until it breaks. By now, the deer was long gone, having been scared off by the newcomer. I stare up at the person and open my mouth to speak, but, before I could even get a word out, they climb up the nearest tree so fast, I hardly blinked by the time they had perched themselves on a sturdy branch.

I could only stare in amazement at the being as they stare back at me— Well, at least I think they are. Their face is covered by a wooden mask made from tree bark. It has a small, pointed nose, similar to an owl's beak, while the eyeholes are curved, horizontal slits that keep me from seeing the eyes of the stranger. Looking at their attire, I note that they overall resemble an owl with both their outfit and posture. The person tilts their head sharply in an unnatural manner that makes me flinch. I nervously crawl back with my heart beating out of my chest, moving slowly under their gaze until I'm hidden by the bushes. I then scramble to my feet and book it, not caring that I had left both of my weapons behind. I take refuge in my cave, but was too afraid to leave, even to get water. I mean, what if they're still out there?

'Who was that?' I wonder while bringing my knees to my chest and sigh. It was the same person from when I first came here, I'm sure of it, but why are they dressed like that?

'Have they been following me, or was that just a coincidence? Are they good, or are they bad?' My mind was plagued with questions about the stranger even as the night came. I was hungry, thirsty and severely paranoid, but I wasn't about to leave now. It's too dark outside anyway.

I release a shriek when a body suddenly drops down from the roof of the cave and crawl into the space deeper as they slowly stand from their crouched, landing position. Their posture remains slouched as they gaze into my temporary home with their hands cupped in front of them. I find myself nervous, not knowing what they were hiding, and press against the cave wall as they come nearer. My body trembles with each soft step they take closer before the person kneels to my seated height and holds out their hands to me. I look down as they open to show what's inside and note the black nails that are pointed like talons as well as the thin, yet calloused fingers that reveal to me a small dead mouse.

My stomach twists in disgust, feeling revolted by the sight of the rodent. I never liked mice or rats. I find them repulsive. Their head tilts in confusion at my disgusted reaction before they set the mouse down at my feet. I bring my legs closer to my chest to keep them away from the small creature as though it'd come back to life and race up my pant leg. The stranger then stands up and leaves without saying a word.

I keep my gaze on their back as they disappear into the foggy night, and when they're gone, I shove the mouse aside with my shoe with a cringe. No way am I eating that. It's too small anyway. It'd be only a bite of meat with a ton of bones. I groan softly and lie down before trying to sleep away the hunger pains.

I just want this day to end.

Man of the Woods

- -

• Y/N: Your Name

— — — — — — — — — — — — — — — — — Y o u r

POV:_____

_____

My eyes felt as though they had been glued shut as I pry the lids open to greet the morning, my mind still feeling exhausted, even after my peaceful rest. My body aches from the position I had laid in as I force myself to sit up and stretch my limbs. Afterwards, I run a hand through my hair only to feel disgusted by it's greasy texture.

'I should bathe in the stream at some point.' Though I'd love to feel clean again, there was a concern hanging over my head. What if that person shows up again? What if they're watching me? I'd be too paranoid to properly wash myself. I find myself surprised when I look over to my left. Sitting there, on the ground beside me, is a thin slab of bark, which acts as a plate for the hefty amount of blackberries that sat in a messy pile on the wood.

'Did they put this here?' I wonder anxiously, knowing that the stranger had likely returned while I had been asleep. I bring the bark onto my folded legs and hesitate to bring one of the berries to my lips. They don't look out of the ordinary to me and don't appear to be tampered with in any way.

My stomach growls in anger at my tease, causing me to sigh as I pop the first berry into my mouth, which instantly began watering at the taste. As I do this, I take notice that the mouse the being had brought yesterday has disappeared, so I think they must've taken it. Just as I reach for another blackberry, the sound of a flute plays from right outside the cave, causing me to jump in fright and nearly knock over the rest of the fruits. My body instinctively trembles as I crane my neck to peer out the mouth of the cave, and I tense upon spotting a figure sitting on a branch of one of the nearby trees. In their hands is the instrument I hear, but they're too far up to distinguish any features not hidden by their mask.

I bite back the pain of my hunger as my stomach accompanies the soft sound of the flute with ungodly growls, and I look back at the berry in my hand. It physically hurt to stare at it, so I quickly pop it into my mouth like the last one before hurriedly devouring the rest. I couldn't seem to restrain myself. They tasted so good! I wish I had savored them more. Even when the bark was left empty, my stomach yearned for more food. It wasn't enough, but it certainly helped.

I rub the back of my sore neck as I peer over to the pile of wood I have stacked neatly in a pile. I want to make more weapons to hunt with and some traps, if I can manage, but I also need to make a fire.

These are things I can't keep putting off. I stand up and dust off my clothes before grabbing the rock I use to collect water. By then, the music had stopped, leaving only the chirping of birds to fill the air as I poke my head out to look around. I can't see them anymore.

'Did they leave?' I would've felt relieved had I not felt a burning stare directed at me. I may not be able to see them, but they are definitely still watching. I take a deep breath before stepping out and walking towards the stream. I was sure it would rain soon, as the air was heavy and muggy, the scent of it hanging in the air. I'll have to find a better means of collecting water, then, since rain water is much cleaner than what's in the stream. Eventually, I reach my destination and have a drink before bringing what I could back to the cave. I, then, set out in search of sticks that would make for good firewood while keeping an eye on the dreary sky.

'It always so gloomy here,' I note before realizing I no longer felt eyes on me. I hum and make my way back when my arms are full of sticks. I'm stunned to find even more wood placed in front of the cave and immediately peer up into the trees. The supplier of the sticks stares down at me from the same branch they were perched on before, causing me to back up towards the cave, as though it would protect me. The figure did not move, which eased me slightly, but it was still unsettling to be stared at so intensely.

I suppose I should be grateful, though. They did bring me food and firewood. I drop off my findings before setting out again, picking up more flammable things to burn. To take a break, I lean against a pine tree, but immediately pull away when my fingers touch something sticky. I smile at the sight of sap, knowing that it's something useful to me, but then, I feel something wet drip onto my nose.

I gaze up and see that it's beginning to rain, so I'll have to collect the sap some other time. I will have to keep this area in mind. I race back to the cave, not wanting the twigs I found to get soaked, and pant heavily to catch my breath when I get there. I take a seat and form a small pile of wood before grabbing a stick and drilling it into another using my hands.

"Come on. Come on," I mutter under my breath, feeling motivated at the sight of smoke created by the friction. I spin the stick faster, ignoring the pain in my hands, even though I know I had gotten a splinter or two, and cheer in success when I manage to get a small blaze going.

"Yes!" I smile widely and blow softly on the flames to get it to spread and grow bigger. I, then, relax, tucking my knees to my chest and hugging them tight as I listen to the calming sounds of the dripping rain and the crackling fire. Curious, I peer outside to check on my stalker, and sure enough, they're still up in that tree, getting wetter by the second. I wonder why they aren't trying to seek shelter rather than spy on me and begin to feel a bit bad. Sure, they seem a bit scary, but it's not like they did anything bad to me— Well, other than push me, that is.

"H- Hey!" I shout, successfully gaining their attention. "You can come in here if you'd like. It's better than getting soaked out there." They don't say anything in response and are still for a moment, as though they had contemplated my offer, before the person descends from the massive oak. Their movements are similar to that of an animal as they use all four limbs to climb the branches with their face pointed downwards. Soon enough, they drop onto the muddy forest floor and enter with great hesitance.

'Funny. Shouldn't I be the one scared right now?' I scoot over to have the fire between us and wait for them to come closer. The distance is kept as they sit cross-legged across from me before shaking their head like a dog to remove water, sending droplets flying all over the place. The figure gradually relaxes their shoulders the longer we sit in silence, but the atmosphere was uncomfortable, so I spoke to break the tension.

"Who are you?" I question softly, to which they answer with silence. They didn't even glance my way, only stared at the fire. "Hello? Can you speak?" I wave a hand near their face, being weary of the small flame that threatened to snag the fabric of my clothes, causing the person to jump back a bit. I quickly retract my hand and apologize. "Sorry... Thank you for helping me out," I say, hoping to make them more comfortable. They simply nod and move back to their spot before sticking their claws out towards the fire to warm them.

"Why are you here, human?" Spoke a gentle and polite voice that held a masculine quality to it. The question caught me off guard and caused me to stutter.

"I... I, um..." After getting a grip, I relax my hold on my knees and vaguely say with a light frown, "It was the closest place I could run to."

"It has been many years since a human has come to this land. Forgive me for coming off a bit wary. Your kind has a habit of making a mess of things." His words sounded insulting, regardless of their light quality, but I was confused by him saying "your kind", as though he isn't human himself. He is human, isn't he? The doubt beginning to creep into my mind put me on edge. He had the body of a human, from what I can tell, even with his odd nails, but the way he moves is strangely animalistic.

"Well, I guess you're not wrong..." I trail off, trying to think of what to say next. He doesn't seem very thrilled about me being here. "B-But, you shouldn't have much to worry about with me."

"I beg to differ," he quickly cuts in, causing me to flinch. "You've already disrupted things." I gulp and hang my head, feeling like I should be ashamed. The man takes notice of this and speaks in a softer tone. "I have stopped your mistakes thus far, however, so it's fine."

"If I'm so much trouble, I'll hide elsewhere." I stand abruptly, upset and somewhat willing to leave, even though the rain storm is raging on outside.

"Hide?" He tilts his head, sounding concerned. "From what?" My fists clenches and unclenches as I breathe out a sigh and sit back down, realizing how childish my outburst was. I'm just so on edge in front of this stranger. I shuffle uncomfortably on the ground and stare into the fire with a heavy heart. It's not like I mind telling anybody about my situation, but I'm worried he might send me home if I do. My silence causes him to speak up again. "I will try to be understanding." I glance up at the masked figure and bite the inside of my cheek lightly.

"I ran away."

"From where?" He asks softly.

"Home."

"Why?" He continues to pry, causing my heart to ache a bit.

"I just... I couldn't take the pressure anymore. Why am I even telling you this? I don't even know you. It's not like you actually care." I glare at the dancing flame and, once again, hug my knees to my chest.

"For the moment, you have taken residence in my territory. I care for anything in my domain within reason."

'His domain? Is this forest his, then?' I wasn't fully convinced he actually cared to know the reason. I imagine he's more curious than anything. He'll probably call me stupid once I tell him. Regardless, I expose my problem.

"My mother always pushed me for greatness, having high expectations, but I can't do that anymore. She pushes too hard, and I... I don't even want what she was trying to get me to achieve. We yelled at each other, and it got kind of ugly. I just wanted to go away for a while. I know it's a stupid reason, but I just..." My bottom lip quivers and my voice had wavered greatly as my eyes start to water. I bury my face in my arms to escape his gaze and do my best to hold back a sob. I don't like to cry in front of people, let alone in front of strangers. I'm just so stressed; I couldn't help it. I hear the shuffling of clothes as the man moves in closer, causing me to glance up. My head perks and leans back in surprise when I find his mask mere centimeters from my face.

"You needn't cry. I don't find your reason, as you say, 'stupid'." My breath caught in my throat as sharp, black talons gingerly brush the skin of my cheek with care. His fingers hardly made any contact, and he stood from his crouched position immediately after. "I bid you goodnight, human. You are more than welcome to stay, but I warn you: please, do not disrupt my forest. I've worked very hard to keep it at peace." I nod my head in understanding, relieved that he'd be letting me stay.

"I get it. I'll try not to be much of a nuisance. Thank you. Do you have a name by any chance?" The male nods and answers with,

"Of course I do. I am Owen, King of Owls and guardian of this forest." My eyes grow wide in disbelief upon hearing his title.

'King of Owls... Just like that old story. It couldn't be true, right?' I brush it off, but clearly hold doubt on my countenance.

"Owen? Sounds similar to owl to me," I say as a way of humoring him, and unbeknownst to me, a smile twitched into place under his mask.

"Yes, I suppose it does. Do you have a title, human?"

"Y/N... Just Y/N." I'm no one special. I hold no notable title, and I hardly regard my family name as anything important anymore. I am just a girl, a human girl who's a nobody. That is what I'm happiest as. The masked man nods his head before returning to the trees outside. It was then I realized the rain had stopped.

'Maybe he prefers the trees to the ground?' I look back to my dying fire and feed the flames a few more sticks just to admire its dance for a little while longer.

'King of Owls, huh?' A smile finds it's way to my lips and I let out a light laugh.

'That's impossible.'

Bird Bath

● Y/N: Your Name

— — — — — — — — — — — — — — — — Y o u r

POV:_____

_____

Brown boots trudge through the mud of the gloomy forest while Y/N's mind was lost in thought. She still kept in mind where she was going, so that she wouldn't actually lose herself amongst the trees, but right now, she was mostly focused on trying to relax. Surviving out in the wilderness felt so tiring, but there was no desire to go home just yet. She starts to notice the increase of stones as she heads up a hill, finding them in a wide variety of shapes and colors, and stops.

'Maybe this is far enough?' She sighs softly and looks up at the surrounding trees, her ears picking up the sound of splashing water. The noise wasn't consistent, so she ruled out the possibility of a waterfall, but that only made her curiouser.

'Maybe there's an animal nearby?' She has no weapons on her at the moment, but still, she was curious to know the source of the sound, so she follows her ears. Soon enough, she happens upon a tree whose branches are decorated with a thick, feathered cloak, brown pants and a familiar, wooden mask. Y/N's brows scrunch as she holds her hand out and touches the rough bark of the mask before hearing another splash. After taking a few steps further in, she yelps and slaps both her hands over her gaping mouth as her cheeks burn brighter than the sun.

Sitting in a large, natural hot spring is a naked owl king, who's back is turned to her. His body and shaggy brown hair dripped with water as steam rose off the surface of the pool. The embarrassed squeal she let out quickly caught Owen's attention and caused him to whip his head around unnaturally far. It did not make a full 180, but it was still more than any human could spin their head. Y/N didn't catch this, however, for she had already gone running and hid behind the nearest tree, her heart hammering in her chest. She did her best to slow her breathing as she presses her forehead against the bark and closes her eyes.

"Y/N, is that you? What are you doing over there?" Asks the brunette in his signature soft voice with a gentle smile on his lips as he stares at the tree she hid behind. He found it amusing, like she was playing a game of hide-and-seek with him. He just spotted her before she could get a hiding spot.

"I'm so sorry! I didn't mean to disturb you!" She apologizes pro-
fusely, really not intending to disturb his bath time. She tried to will
herself to leave, but her legs felt glued to the ground.

"You aren't disturbing me at all. Come here." He ushers kindly,
unknowingly making her face heat up even further.

"No thanks!" She shouts, causing the being to chuckle as he stands
up, making the water to leak down his thin, yet muscular, frame. The
mud did not bother him as his feet squished into it, as he was used to
walking barefoot around the forest, and besides, there are plenty of
stones to keep them from getting too dirty. When he walks around
the tree where Y/N stands, he finds her pressed up against it with her
body tensed up and eyes shut tight. Owen didn't quite understand
why she gave off the appearance of being afraid, though, it did make
him feel concerned, so he puts a gentle hand on the girl's shoulder.

The contact makes her jump and turn around, which she instantly
realized was a mistake, since she was now face to face with the naked
king. Her response caused him to flinch back as well. She blushed
madly and was quick to lock eyes with him to avoid accidentally look
down at his body. Staring at his face might be embarrassing, but not
as much as catching a glimpse of... that. The man's skin holds a light
tan, but it was clear that he did not often show himself in the sun,
and a shadow of stubble coats his chin and jaw. His most defining
feature, however, had to be the giant, apricot-orange orbs with wide
pupils that stare right down into her soul. They were so pretty, she
could get lost in them forever; in fact she found herself enchanted by
them until Owen spoke and snapped her out of it.

"Why don't you come join me? It looks as though you can use a good soak." He didn't realize how wrongly his words sounded to the young lady. It was only an offer to let her bathe, since she had gone many days without cleaning herself. Dirt caked her skin and tangled hair. Even her clothes are all filthy from having to sleep on the ground. The thing is, the offer is to bathe with him, so she was quick to decline.

"Oh, no, no, no! I have to, um... Collect some food anyway. M-Maybe some other time?" She says frantically with a crooked smile while holding up her hands and slowly backing away from the creature. She stops, however, when he gives a princely smile and holds out his hand for her to take. All she could do was stare at it.

"I won't bite. I'll assist you with finding something to eat afterwards. I can show you the blackberry bushes." She felt conflicted. Obviously, she didn't want to bathe with some strange man, who she knows nothing about, but he didn't seem like he was trying to take advantage of her, and besides, she does need help finding food. She hasn't had much luck in that department so far and, not to mention, how badly she needs a bath. Heaving a sigh, Y/N swallows her pride.

"F- Fine, but don't look, okay?" She grips her arms, already feeling self-conscious about her body and she didn't even take her clothes off yet. Owen's head tilts as he retracts his hand back to his side. Him being attractive didn't exactly help things either.

'How embarrassing,' she thought while turning her face away from him.

"As you wish." The man walks past to go back into the hot spring and settles into the water before peering back at her with expectant eyes.

"I said don't look," she snaps with narrowed eyes, leading Owen to arch a brow and switch his gaze to the other side of the pool.

"I don't see the issue." Y/N breathes a sigh before peeling off her clothes, but she keeps on her bra and underwear, since she was not comfortable going fully nude, unlike the man in the pool. She was thankful that he kept his eyes respectfully averted as she stepped into the pool and instantly felt her worries slip away as she sat in the steaming liquid.

"Must I sit like this the entire time?" The idea seemed to irritate him just slightly. Having to look one direction for the entire bath didn't sound relaxing at all to him. After crossing her arms over her chest and putting one leg over the other, she says,

"You can look, I guess. Just don't stare." She receives a quick glance as he moves his head forward, causing her to hold herself tighter while sinking deeper into the water. At last, it clicked.

"Are you embarrassed?" He questions with a slight grin.

"No, I'm holding myself like this because it's comfortable," she retorts in a sarcastic tone. He chuckles at her response and admires the scenery ahead.

"You weren't out looking for food, were you?" Y/N shakes her head.

"No, just... exploring, but I wasn't lying about needing to get some. All I've eaten were those berries you left for me yesterday." Owen gives a slight nod and shuts his eyes as the sun starts to peek through the clouds to cast it's light onto the duo. They stay in peaceful silence, listening to the forest sounds around them until an idea pops into the man's head.

With a mischievous smile, he takes a deep breath before submerging himself entirely underwater. Y/N yelps in surprise when he resurfaces right in front of her. He had come so close that she could feel the heat radiating off his body as he raises his cupped hands and dumps water over her head. He gave a childish giggle when she squealed and shut her eyes to keep the liquid out, which caused her to frown at him when she opened them again. He sinks back into the water, leaving his large eyes to peek over the surface as they sparkle with delight.

Cracking a sly smirk, she gets back at him by splashing the water in his face, causing the man to shoot his head out of the water and shake it while laughing. He was quick to retaliate with another splash aimed right at her, and in that moment, all tensions fade away as laughter filled the air. Y/N lost herself in the fun as the two of them went back and forth, splashing at each other until they both grew tired. A smile stayed on their faces, however, even after it was done. Owen has never played with a human before.

He found it quite fun. The animals in the forest never really returned his playful antics the way she had. As for Y/N, she was glad to have a moment where all her troubles disappeared. It had been so long since she had let loose. It felt freeing.

The forest guardian sighs in content as he shuts his bright eyes and basks in the peace that had fallen over them. The girl had no clue how long she had been there, but if she had to guess, it was now late in the afternoon. Night should fall soon, but she didn't want to head back to the cave just yet. Y/N sends her company a quick glance before asking out of the blue, "Why did you save that deer?"

"What do you mean?" The man cocks his head at her, staring directly into her eyes, which made her self-conscious thoughts return. She crosses her arms back over her chest before staring out at the horizon to avoid his piercing gaze.

"You killed a mouse for me, but you wouldn't let me have the deer."

"The doe has children. They're far too young to survive without their mother, so I couldn't just let you kill her. The mouse, however, held no purpose. Nothing would be harmed by its death," he justifies. She gives a light hum and nods her head in understanding.

"Oh, that makes sense. I'm sorry for causing trouble."

"It is fine. No damage was done." She heaves a soft sigh before standing up.

"I should be heading back. It's getting late." The man frowns in disappointment, wishing the human would keep him company for just a bit longer.

"Very well, then. I will stop by to help you soon." Y/N ignores his stare as she quickly throws on her clothes and cringes at the feel of them sticking to her wet skin. She didn't want to catch a cold in this weather and wanted to hide her form from Owen, even though he didn't seem to be having any perverse thoughts while looking at her. Once she's ready, she turns and bows her head to the man.

"Thank you." There was a faint heat that spread across her cheeks as she walked away, while the male sighs at her retreating form. The dreary clouds return to cover the sky as he sinks back into the water in thought for a few more minutes before coming out as well. He shakes out his hair while stepping out of the pool, causing the brown locks to puff out a bit as he steps closer to where he left his clothes. There was an unfamiliar warmth in his chest as he slipped on his pants and threw on his cloak when his thoughts drifted to the human girl who invaded his homeland.

'Perhaps, it won't be so bad having her around?'

Attention, Attention

A uthor's Note:

Please listen, for I have a very important announcement to make. As of right now, all of my books are going to be put on hold. No, it's not because I hate you and want to make you suffer by leaving you to wait for what's going to happen next, though, that does sound like something I'd do. (I'm kidding of course. I'd never do that to you guys.) I have a very good reason for doing this, and no, it isn't due to health issues or anything like that.

I'm doing this because I want to go back and edit all of my books. Now, in case you didn't notice, I've made many, many books. It's made it difficult to both edit and post new chapters at the same time, so I'm going to slow it down and do one thing at a time. I will be continuing my author's notebook: The Golden Throne, for that book in particular doesn't take up much time or effort. But, anyway this is how it's gonna go down:

I'm going to start with the books I've all ready marked as completed, then work my way to my unfinished stories. Once an unfinished book is done with the editing process, it will continue with new chapters. Now, I highly recommend you be patient with this process, for it might take quite a bit of time to do, but I do have a reward in store for when I finish editing everything. I will be putting up, not one, but two new books for you guys to read. There will also be another benefit to the editing, for it will refresh my memory on the story and probably give me new ideas for the next chapters.

Thank you for listening to me and reading my books. I'll be sure to work as quickly as I can to get through all my books while properly editing, so you won't have to wait too long. I really appreciate you guys.

~Golden~

Blackberry Bushes

_____Author's
__ Note:_____

Hello, everybody!

Welcome back to King of Owls. I hope you're as excited as I am to start back up again. If you'd like to have a look at the newly edited chapters, be my guest! If not, that's fine too. I won't take up too much of your time. I'm sure you'd like to get started. I just want to thank you all for your support and patience. I really am lucky to have such a wonderful audience.

~Here we go~

_____

•Y/N: Your Name

_____—Author's
POV:_____

_____

The rustle of leaves disturbs the peaceful silence of the forest as a figure jumps from branch to branch at lightning speed, seeming as though they were gliding to each tree with every stride. The heavy cloak of feathers adorning their lithe body wasn't even enough to slow them down as they travel towards the human's cave. Owen didn't wish to keep Y/N waiting with the sun threatening to set soon, even though his large eyes could see perfectly well in the darkness. He knows a human's eyes were not so strong, and besides, the fog always sets in at night, which would only make things more complicated for the girl. The near-silent flapping of wings sound on both sides of him as a parliament of owls join him in his journey.

It wasn't uncommon of the birds to accompany him near nightfall and even sometimes during the day. Though normally owls weren't animals that flock together in large groups, they were always naturally drawn to his presence, which was only fitting for a man with the title of King of Owls. Soon enough, they reach their destination, and the man launches himself out of the trees before landing gracefully on top of the cave. He crouches down on all fours before crawling towards the opening and dropping onto the grass below, which causes Y/N to jump in surprise at his sudden appearance and drop the stick she was using to start a fire. Her frantic heart calms when she sees her visitor is no threat.

"Don't do that! You nearly gave me a heart attack." She sighs while resting a hand over her chest.

"Forgive me, that was not my intention," he apologizes while drawing nearer. "I've come to take you to the berry bushes, as we've planed."

"Right." The girl pushes herself off the ground before dusting off her filthy clothes. She takes a mental note to wash them in the river at some point. "I was actually worried you weren't gonna show with how late it's gotten."

"Why wouldn't I?" Owen tilts his head to the side. "We had a deal, did we not?"

"Most people I know don't keep promises and deals," she mutters.

"That is what differs between me and humans. I do not tell lies or break promises." His words made her smile slightly, since they sounded sincere.

"I hope so. Well, let's head out before it gets dark." Y/N walks past the unusual man, still convinced that he was human and not some "King of Owls", like he claims to be.

"Right." He nods before following after her into the woods. "I'd hate for you to get lost in the night."

"You don't have to worry much about that. I'm pretty good with knowing where I'm at and where I'm going. I have a good memory," she claims while poking at the side of her head.

"That's good, nonetheless, I will make sure you find your way there and back well. There are some creatures I might have to keep at bay in order to grant you safe passage." The man is confused when the human chuckles, and his head cocks to the side.

"You talk funny."

"Do I?"

"Yeah, really sophisticated, but I like it. It's different than what I'm used to." The forest guardian smiles underneath his mask, unbeknownst to the girl beside him.

"I like how you sound too. Though, I especially like it when your face turns red, like it did at our bath." Y/N chokes on air as her cheeks burn bright red at his comment, which brings out a light laugh from the creature. "Yes, like that. I think it's funny."

"Stop talking." She felt tempted to pick up a stick and throw it at his head. Had he not been kind enough to help her, she would've. A smug look remains on his hidden features as she shakes her head at him. The rest of their long journey is spent in comfortable silence as they took in the sounds of crickets, cicadas and croaking frogs.

At times, Y/N would gaze up at the trees and spot a few owls peering down at them with their wide eyes, which she still found unnerving, but they weren't hurting anybody. The two march up a hill, and by that point, she was ready to collapse, but her exhausted wore off the second she laid eyes on the many bushes of blackberries at the top, and behind them, are a few mulberry and crabapple trees. The mere sight of food made her mouth water and her stomach growl in hunger.

"Take as much as you need. I'll help you carry it back to your den." Y/N tears her gaze away from the bountiful supply of fruits to give her guide a grateful smile.

"Thank you." Not wasting another second, she ran to the bushes before picking all the ripe blackberries she could find before shoving them into her mouth to satisfy her hunger. She was starving. Owen observes while stepping towards the trees and having a seat beneath one to wait. The human didn't seem very threatening in comparison to ones he had encountered in the past, which he was thankful for.

It makes it easier to keep her out of trouble. A saw-whet owl flaps its wings and jumps out of the crabapple tree Y/N reaches into before deciding to land on Owen's shoulder. The bird coos and bites at his mask in a request for attention, so he brings a gentle finger to the creatures head to pet it. The girl fashions a sling using her green sweater jacket before putting all the fruits she had gathered into it to free her hands. She wished to take everything, but knew that wouldn't be wise.

The berries wouldn't keep for very long, and there are plenty to come back and grab later. As she busies herself with that, Owen stares at the horizon, viewing the seemingly never-ending forest. If one looked close enough, however, they could notice a slight blur on the far side of the woods, where the rift exists. The entrance is small and hard to see for most. It definitely takes a keen eye even when standing right in front of it. It is especially rare for a human to spot it, and yet, here he is, looking after one that had ventured into his world. His attention is captured when Y/N sits at his side to give her legs a break, her stomach no longer in pain from the emptiness now that it had been filled.

"Did you get enough?" He asks as the owl on his shoulder takes off in search of something to eat.

"Yes, thank you. I was starving. Finding food was a lot harder than I thought it was gonna be, so I really appreciate your help." He bows his head in acknowledgment to her thanks before looking back at the setting sun. It wouldn't be long now before night fell, but he was surprised by the lack of fog at his feet. There's always a dense fog at night and the sky is usually so clouded, but today, it's mostly clear. He found it odd.

"So, what's with the mask?" Y/N's question drug him out of his thoughts and brought his attention back to her.

"It's easier to hunt this way. It helps me blend in with the trees."

"But, you aren't hunting right now. Wouldn't you be more comfortable without it? You can take it off."

"I suppose." Reaching behind his head, Owen unties the string before setting the mask on the ground beside him. His hand stays on top of it, though, and his gaze lingers on the covering, a soft pang striking his heart.

"Did you make it?"

"No, my father did."

"Your father?"

"Yes, he passed a long time ago," he says quietly, making Y/N regret her question.

"Oh... I'm sorry."

"Don't be. He was a good guardian and a very kind father. He passed this forest down to me, so I do what I can to take care of it and it's inhabitants."

"May I ask how he died?" His eyes dimmed a little as the sun almost full disappeared in the horizon, the fog steadily setting in, at last, though, it was not thick.

"My kind lives very long lives, much longer than any human. We can live on for centuries, but we are not invincible. There was a man— A human man, who found this place. He came to hunt the beasts that roam here, and my father would not stand for it. He ripped this strange stick from the man's hands, but..." The muscles in his jaw tighten as his bottom lip quivers.

"He took it back, and the stick let out a loud noise. The next I knew, my father was on the ground, covered in blood." Y/N's eyes grow wide as she covers her mouth in shock. It's no wonder he had been so weary of her at first. She was left speechless, though, she wished to comfort the man who shuts his eyes and lowers his head. "I drove the trespasser out by calling on the owls, but it was too late to save my father. I still think of him even though so much time has passed." With a gentle sigh, his sharp nails trace over the bark of the mask with a longing look in his orange eyes. He missed him.

"I... I'm so sorry. That's awful. No one should ever have to experience something like that."

"It is why I want to keep an eye on you. Personally, I don't think you're very dangerous, but I will be cautious, nonetheless. I don't trust humans, not fully."

"That's okay, I understand. If I were in your place, I'd probably be the same way. To be honest, I don't trust humans either, but my reasons are a bit different. I'm glad you don't think I'm that bad. I don't want to be any trouble to you, especially since you've been so nice... Hey, Owen?"

"Yes?"

"Why do you keep referring to yourself as something nonhuman? If you aren't, then what are you?"

Nest of Twigs and Vine

● Y/N: Your Name

_____Author's

POV:_____

_____

"That is because I am not human, Y/N," answers the man while lifting his head to lock eyes with the girl. "I am a creature of this forest, same as my ancestors. Though, it is only me now." Owen's feet shuffle as he rolls his shoulders, puffing his chest a bit. He, then, looks to the horizon, but Y/N was not satisfied yet. Aside from his abnormally large eyes, there didn't seem to be anything inhuman about him.

"But, you seem human to me," she insists. "Are you sure you're anything else? If your family has lived here for centuries, then maybe, it's just that their senses adapted to the landscape. That might explain a longer life too." She tries to be logical about it, unconvinced he could be anything else. The teen is surprised to hear a delicate laugh as the man gets to his feet before peering down at her.

"You don't believe me?" He tilts his head sharply, causing her to give him an apologetic look.

"Sorry, it just doesn't make sense to me." He hums, moving his head back into place.

"Then, perhaps, I should show you?" Y/N didn't know what he meant by that and watches with intrigue as she stands as well, cradling the fruit she gathered in her arms. Owen takes some steps back before shedding his cloak to reveal his bare torso. He man rolls his shoulders and neck, the skin on his back stretching strangely as he does so, which causes the girl to scrunch her brows. The man emits an odd sort of growl that sounded mixed with a pigeon's coo as boney wings extend upwards towards the sky.

He hunches over, talons ripping at the grass as the flesh of his hands and feet turns grey and scaly with a claw beginning to grow out of the back of his heel. Y/N's first reaction was to cover her mouth, leading her to drop her food. She stumbles back as a mix of brown and creamy white feathers dotted with black spots poke out from his skin and hair aside from his hands, the lower half of his legs and a majority of his face. His legs bend, cracking as they take a different shape, which caused the girl to wince. A massive tail of long feathers fans out from his backside, and while the rest of him turned more birdlike, his face is what kept its human appearance— aside from a few small feathers that form on the sides of his face, under his jaw and a little under his large eyes. It was a gruesome transformation, but the end result was stunning; a little scary, but stunning. Y/N was in awe.

'He was telling the truth.' She lost feeling in her legs and fell back, sitting on the ground in shock. Her eyes were nearly as wide as his as Owen turns to face her while standing up, wings tucked away as he smiles kindly.

"Believe me now?" Y/N was speechless. She could only nod as she scans his body. Her expression makes him laugh as he bends down to retrieve the fallen berries and puts them back in her jacket as he speaks. "I hope you'll forgive me for hiding myself like I did. I thought I might frighten you, and I know humans do rash things when scared."

"Y... You're..." She had no words she could muster, as it was still taking her a minute to process the transformation. She couldn't believe the story was real. The Owl King is real, and he's standing right in front of her. She didn't know why, but it brought tears to her eyes.

"Oh, dear. Was it a mistake to reveal myself?" he asks while tilting head in an inhuman manner, backing up to giver her space because he was worried that he might've scared her. The girl is quick to shake her head and gives him a small smile, filling the man with relief.

"I'm sorry, I just don't know what to say." The birdlike creature chuckles and crawls in closer to fold her jacket, securing the fruits, before fetching his mask and cloak. By the time he was done, the sun had fully set, the dark night stealing the stage with its sparkling stars and brilliant moon.

"Night has fallen. It's a long walk back. Would you like me to fly you to the den, Y/N? It will be faster and much safer too," He offers as the girl stands and dusts herself off.

"Oh, n- no, thank you. I think I'm good," she declines politely while staring at the large wings that had sprouted from his back. Though she was not entirely frightened of the man or his sudden change in physique, the thought of having him fly her anywhere made her a wee bit anxious. Her body goes stiff as he comes in closer, standing only inches from her face with an encouraging smile.

"Don't be shy, now. It's fun, I assure you." He jumps back with the flap of his wings, sending a strong gust of wind her way and making her hair to blow back wildly. He spins around with wings spread wide to present his back to the female, his toes digging into the earth as he crouches down. "I've never carried anyone before, so be sure to hold on tightly. I like going fast and I'd hate for you to fall."

'Well, that was comforting.' She comes closer, moving slow with uncertainty, but stops near the items he had gathered. "What about all this?"

"I can carry those too. I promise, I won't drop them. I have good grip," he assures.

"All right, then," she mutters, reaching a hesitant hand towards his back and placing it between his shoulders. Under the plush feathers lie strong muscles that shift and flex under her touch, causing the wings to move slightly as he patiently waits for the girl to get on. At first, she didn't know how to position herself without pulling on the feathers or risking falling off and awkwardly straddles his back while clinging to his neck. She holds him tighter as he moves, his hands grabbing her legs and adjusting them to wrap around his waist like a belt. With her secure, he crawls over to the pile of things he has to take to fold Y/N's jacket and his mask inside the cloak, using it as a makeshift sack, before grasping it firmly in his claws.

"Are you ready, Y/N?"

"Absolutely not." The owl chuckles as the girl hides her face in the crook of his neck while lightly flapping his wings. This makes her hold strengthen and her eyes shut.

"Off we go!" He shouts excitedly while breaking into a run, flapping his wings harder and harder with every step, causing Y/N's heart to beat like crazy. Every now and again, he jumps, staying airborne longer with each leap until, at last, he takes flight. The ride starts off bumpy as he flies higher into the sky, way above the towering trees before straightening his wings to glide, flapping as often as needed to keep a steady position. Smiling, he looks over at his passenger to view her reaction, but finds her still in the same position as when they took off. "You should open your eyes."

"I'm good, thanks!" She shouts, though it wasn't necessary, since she is close to his ear. He chuckles and tucks in his wings, sending them plummeting to the ground. Y/N screams, heart sinking to her stomach as she dares to sneak a peek, which she instantly regrets. "Pull up! Pull up!" Grinning cheekily, Owen does what she asks, flying back to their previous height. "Maniac," she mutters while cautiously lifting her head. Her lips part in awe as she looks over the forest. She knew it was big, but it was like there was no end. Y/N looks behind, spotting the hill they were on before, but it was already so far away, and as she looked around, she saw no lights from her town or any sign of civilization for that matter, like it had just disappeared into thin air. She didn't know how to feel about that. "It's huge," she says while facing front again. "I didn't realize the forest was this big."

"It goes on forever doesn't it?" Owen shuts his eyes and takes in a calming breath, the fresh air filling his lungs. "I haven't seen a clear night like this in ages." Y/N relaxes her chin on his shoulder and hums.

"Yeah, I suppose the weather has been pretty dreary. You know, this isn't so bad as long as I don't look straight down." The bird man laughs, able to feel her slight tremble as he picks up speed, and decides to take a little detour on their way to the cave. Y/N watches in amazement as they travel over the terrain, spotting massive rock formations, waterfalls and streams that lead up to large lake, and finding all sorts of animals from deer to raccoons, even a large moose. The sights formed a beautiful smile on her face, and at some point, she shut her eyes to relish the feeling of the wind in her hair. When she opens them, she's surprised to find many owls traveling around them, flying in the same direction. Owen tilts his wings, sending them down gradually before landing softly on the ground. Gravity takes ahold of her as she slides off his back, making her a little lightheaded.

"Woah!" Y/N stumbles over her feet and giggles as she flattens her hair, then beams at the Owl King. "That was so cool!" Owen smiles back at her and opens the cloak in his hands to retrieve her jacket of fruit.

"I'm glad you enjoyed it. Forgive me for not bringing you straight here. I haven't enjoyed a long flight like that for a long time."

"Oh, I don't mind. It was scary at first, but you were right. Flying is fun. I'm almost sad we had to come down." She smiles up at the night sky and sighs serenely. Being up there was freeing and made her feel like all her troubles were meaningless. All she was focused on was the beauty of the woods and its inhabitants. Though, a thought came to her as she looks back at the man. "Owen, where do you live?" She inquires, causing him to tilt his head.

"This forest," he answers, confused by her question, which makes her shake her head.

"I mean do you live in a specific place, like how I have this cave?"

"Well, I spend my time everywhere, but I do have something, a nest. Did you want to see it?" He wonders, for why else would she bring it up?

"Well, you don't have to. I was just curious. I always see you outside the cave, so it made me wonder."

"I have no preference of where I sleep, so I don't often spend my time there, but I suppose it's nice to have a home to go to." She smiles sadly and walks inside the cave, Owen following after her.

"It must be nice to feel that way about having a home to go to." He watches as the girl sets down her food by the stack of wood she uses for fires and tilts his head when she sighs. "Every time I think about going home, I just feel depressed." She tenses under his claw as he places it on her shoulder and meets his large eyes. The man then takes her hands and pulls her along, guiding her out of the cave.

"I'd like to show you— if you aren't tired, that is." Y/N shakes her head, feeling a bit giddy to see this nest of his. Once outside, he turns his back to her and lowers himself for the girl to hop on. The human wraps around him, and he takes off as soon as she is ready. She could feel the weight in her chest vanish as they fly through the air once more, Owen becoming a little more daring with his speed now that Y/N knew what to expect, but she did not mind.

The nest was a hard thing to miss once they came close enough. It resides within the twisted branches of an odd and massive tree with a wide trunk. The branches are weaved together with thick vines and flexible twigs, forming a spherical shape with a gaping hole in the side which acts as an entrance. Y/N gasps at the sight of the enormous structure as her guide lands gracefully inside the mouth of the sphere before dropping his cloak and mask on the floor, which is carpeted by a wide array of molted feathers. She slides off the males back and gazes up, straining her eyes to see the owls roosting in smaller nests built in the higher portions of the room. The birds all spin their necks, making noises in greeting to their king. The owls that had been following the two perch on the opening of the large nest and hoot along with the others.

"Wow," she gapes while sitting on the cushioned floor. Owen smiles at this before crawling to the far side of the nest to do his own thing, allowing her to take it all in. Y/N looks out at the night sky, amazed by the things she had experienced today. It was all so surreal. She never expected this sort of thing to happen when she ran away.

She expected to be alone, wallowing in her misery and frustrations to figure things out before going back home, but so much has happened since that first day. There is so much about the world that she doesn't know, like creatures like Owen or the intricacies of this forest. She felt as though she had missed out for years, focusing on things she felt were a waste. There is no interest in going back, not yet, at least. She might never get this chance to experience complete freedom like this ever again. She doesn't ever want it to end.

Little goosebumps form on her skin from the chilly wind that blows into the structure, but she pays no mind to the cold. The gentle sound of a flute catches her attention, causing the girl to turn around. The Owl King sat with his back against the wall with a hand-carved flute in his hands, creating the hypnotic, sleep-inducing music that sent tingles through her body. "Who taught you to play that? Your father?" She wonders making him pause and nod his head.

"My family always loved music, whether it was the whistle of winds rushing through the trees or the pitter-patter of rain against stones. We found it very relaxing." He runs his thumbs over the wood and smiles. "My mother loved to hear me play. She'd dance to the songs with my father, then we'd all take flight to perform in the air."

"But, your songs are so... solemn. How does one dance to that?"

"They are not always. I'm more fond of calming music, is all. Do you not like it?" Y/N shakes her head with a faint smile.

"I find it very soothing. I like when you play it. At first, I found it a little creepy, but I think you are very talented." Smiling to himself, Owen raises the instrument to continue playing, his watchful eyes stuck on his guest, who stares outside. She starts to fall asleep to his song, finding it peaceful here. Her eyes had even shut for a bit until the music came to a stop.

"You are trembling, Y/N. Are you cold?"

"I'm all right. Just keep playing. It's nice." She closes her eyes again when he continues, too tired to hear his near-silent footsteps traveling through the feathers on the floor. Owen stops beside her and takes a seat, never faltering on the notes, before stretching out one of his long legs towards his cloak. The sharp talons snag the feathery fabric and drags it closer to him. The creature paused to drape the cloak over the young woman's body as she goes limp and smiles at her.

He felt a warmth fluttering in his heart as he played throughout the night, never taking his eyes off Y/N as she rested in his nest.

— — — — — — — — — — — — — — — — — —

_____Author's Note:_____

Hello, everyone!

I hope you've all been having a pleasant day and enjoying yourselves. What do you think of the new chapter? I hope you are all pleased with Owen's true form. When I started the story, I did not originally intend on making him look anything like this and was going to make him more humanlike, but as I was editing, I decided to make this change. I think it's more fitting for him.

⇧ ⇧ ⇧

Here's a picture I made of his body to give you a better understanding of it. I have not drawn a picture of his face yet, but I hope to make that soon, so hopefully, you'll get to see that at some point down the line.

Thank you, all, for reading!

~Golden~

Fluffy Feathers

———————————————————Author's
POV:_____

_____

The blissful warmth of sunlight graced Y/N's S/C skin, shining down onto her face and folded arms, which she had rested on throughout the night, breaking her out of her peaceful rest. Groggily, she rubs the sleep out of her eyes and squints as she peers down. The girl panicked after seeing the massive drop below and quickly leaned away from the opening of the nest with a hand over her frantic heart. It takes a moment for her to settle down after the scare.

'Well, that's one way to wake up in the morning.' Sighing, she lies back against the floor cushioned by mountains of feathers and stares up at the ceiling, where she could see some owls slumbering inside smaller nests built into higher parts of the sphere. A few let out quiet sounds, while outside, she could hear the morning birds singing their cheerful song. By turning her head to the side, Y/N finally takes notice of the man who had been beside her, who is still in his birdlike form. Owen's knees are tucked to his chest, while his large wings shield his entire body, including his head.

The only part she could see of him, really, are the sharp talons of his feet. He blended well amongst the feathers and sticks, especially since he sat so still. The human hums, having never seen him sleep before, then takes notice of the cloak beneath her. Sitting up, she pulls it out from under her to examine the cloth in depth. It seems very well made, each feather skillfully woven into the fabric to prevent any from falling out, and if she had to guess, most of them came from him.

She recognized their texture and matched their colors as she ran her fingers over the heavy cloak. He certainly has soft feathers, and they're so simple, yet beautiful all the same. Smiling, Y/N looks over at Owen again to contemplate waking him up, but she didn't wish to disturb his sleep, assuming that he is nocturnal, like most owls, and had stayed up most of the night. There isn't much to keep her occupied, however, and she certainly couldn't get down by herself without dying, so she figures it might be better to go back to sleep for a while longer. Y/N uses a hand to block the sun from getting into her eyes as she seeks a more shady spot to sleep.

It is darker near the back of the nest and on the sides of the opening, where Owen is resting. Not wanting to risk getting into a fight with a territorial owl, she picks herself up and quietly lies beside him in his shadow, using his cloak as a blanket to keep warm. The human then looks up at the creature encased in those big, feathery wings and wonders if he's even comfortable sleeping like that. She clears the thought from her head before shutting her eyes and going back to sleep, which didn't take very long.

About an hour later, Owen awoke, his clawed feet digging into the twigs and feathers on the floor before opening his large, orange eyes. The orbs roll in his skull a bit in a daze as he unfolds his wings and lifts his head from his knees, stretching the limbs upward only to be assaulted by the sunlight. Groaning, he spins himself around to where his back would face the ball of light before getting back into his sleeping position, but he stops before completely covering himself with his wings. He blinks a few times and perks his head to view the sleeping girl at his feet and hums. He had completely forgotten about her being here.

'She changed spots,' he notes, though quickly guessed it was because of the sun. He yawns, his eyelids feeling heavy, but Owen shook his head to wake himself. He is certainly not a morning creature. He much preferred waking up as early as late afternoon, but ever since Y/N had shown up, his sleep schedule has been all over the place. He would have went right back to sleep, but was sure the girl wouldn't want to be stuck in a tree all day until he woke again.

"Human, wake up," he calls, crawling over her sleeping form and lightly shaking her shoulder. "Y/N, I should bring you to your den." The teenager groans and opens her eyes. It took her a moment to become fully alert after seeing his face only inches from her own and instinctively stuck out her hands to push at his chest. He complies, giving her more space, but continues to hover over her, which didn't help to settle her rapid heartbeat.

"That's twice I've been jump-scared this morning," she claims, speaking to herself, while rubbing her eyes.

"Forgive me. I am tired as well, but I think it'll be best if I put you on the ground now so that you aren't trapped up here all day."

"Right," she grumbles while getting out from under him to stand, leaving the cloak on the floor. "That's probably a good idea. I'm getting kinda hungry." He nods in understanding before turning his back to her so that she can climb on. Y/N moves lethargically, her body not as awake as her mind, and holds onto him tight.

"Ready, Y/N?" She merely hums, positioning her face against his neck, where his softest feathers lie. He also had this unidentifiable smell to him that almost smelled like nothing at all, and yet, it was pleasant. She could've fallen asleep right there on his shoulder if he hadn't jumped out right that second. Her body jolted awake as she gave a shout, holding onto him tighter until he steadies himself.

"I hate when you do that." She can hear him laughing to himself as they travel to her cave and land right in front of it. "Thanks for the ride," she says while coming off his back, and he bows his head.

"My plea... sure." His momentary pause made her raise a brow. Owen was no longer looking at her, rather at what's behind her, so she hurriedly spins around. She didn't see anything out of the ordinary, however, until she looked down. The girl gulps when her eyes land on some rather big bear tracks leading into the cave and backs up towards the Owl King. He moves in front of her, walking in first without fear, while she was hesitant to follow behind. To her relief, the place was empty, although she did groan after finding her jacket all torn up and empty of fruit.

"It ate everything," she sighs and shakes her head, picking up the tattered remains of her jacket. "And my jacket's ruined."

"Must've been hungry," he notes. Y/N's face pales when she realizes she might've had to face the bear if she hadn't gone to Owen's nest last night. No longer did she feel safe in this cave.

"What am I suppose to do if it comes back?" she asks worriedly, dropping the jacket onto the ground. It held no use anymore except for maybe scraps for a fire.

"I'll take care of it, don't worry. I'll make sure your den won't be disturbed. Just stay here for now."

"Okay," Y/N seats herself on the hard ground already missing the nest's soft flooring and watches Owen leave without further instruction. She wonders what he will do. She imagined it would be a peaceful approach, considering how kind he is to the animals here. She just hoped the bear wouldn't attempt to hurt him, but something told her it won't. When the Owl King returns, he come bearing thick branches of pine, which he leans up around the mouth of the cave. He had dug holes before placing them inside and covering the base with dirt to secure them into place. Next, he digs a line of holes in front of the opening before filling them with more branches facing outward at an angle, forming a sort of cage.

The spaces between the wooden bars would be enough to let her through, but not anything bigger. Using more sticks and mud, the branches are strongly secured into place. He had even tested their strength by climbing onto them then pulling and pushing at each individual branch until he was certain they would not budge under his weight. Y/N watches with intrigue as he works, amazed by how much he could carry. Those branches were certainly heavy too. To finish off his project, he ties a few feathers to every branch, leaving them to blow gently in the breeze, before squeezing past the bars to walk up to the teen.

"That should do it. My scent alone should detour the animals away from you, but the branches are an extra defense. It may not work on everything though, so I'll be sure to stay close should you ever need my help. I can hear from very far, so call to me if you need assistance."

"Thank you, Owen. I feel safer already." Y/N smiles up at him, noting how sleepy he is. "You should get some rest," she suggests while standing up. "I should be all right on my own for a while. I'm going to get more fruits, since the bear ate all mine. Will I see you again soon, though?" Owen smiles and nods his head before taking some steps back.

"Stay safe, Y/N." The girl waves him goodbye as he slips through the bars before stretching out his wings. She sighs, watching him take off and disappear into the sky, and licks her lips, feeling a little parched.

'Maybe I should get some water before heading to the hill?' With her plan in mind, she sets off. Once Owen reaches his nest, he gives a great yawn and stretches his wings, his eyes fluttering shut as he walks towards a dark place to sleep. He stops when his foot snags on his cloak and looks down at the piece of clothing with a sharply tilted head.

'Poor girl. If the nights get cold, she won't have a jacket anymore to warm her,' he thinks to himself, recalling her torn up jacket. Bending down, he takes the cloak in his claws and runs his scaly fingers over the feathers.

'She seemed to enjoy sleeping here too. Though, I suppose that's because it's much comfier than sleeping on the dirt.' For a moment, he considered letting her live here, but that wouldn't work too well. With the nest so high, she would be unable to leave anytime she wanted. She had no wings to carry her.

Besides, he was not here often, as he didn't have much of a reason to. Sometimes, he travels to the far ends of the forest, as though it even had any ends, and before Y/N came along, he was always busy watching the portals leading into her world along with helping animals if they were in trouble. She could not depend on him to always bring her down to the forest floor. Still, he thinks he would've liked to share his home with her. A trill builds in his throat as he wraps himself up in his wings, holding the cloak to him and shutting his eyes.

'Perhaps she would like a cloak of her own?'

Warmth of a Cloak

● Y/N: Your Name

————————————————————Your

POV:_____

_____

With a tired groan, I rub my weary eyes and shift a little closer to the fire to keep warm. It is yet another cold, rainy day, and unfortunately, I have no jacket to keep me warm anymore, so my only hope is the fire, but the heat is seriously drying out my eyes. A few days have passed since the bear had invaded my hideaway, but thankfully, it hasn't come back. Seems Owen's defenses work well. Sadly, I haven't heard or seen from him lately either, but there have been plenty of owls around to keep watch on me. What I once thought to be an eerie presence I now find quite comforting. The days are getting colder, it seems. It makes me wish I had come out here more prepared.

'Maybe I should just go back home?' Closing my eyes, I shake the thought from my head. I sometimes wonder if mom is sad that her precious "can-do-no-wrong" daughter is gone. Likely, she just misses showing me off to her friends, acting like she's the best parent in the world. The very thought makes my blood boil.

'No, not yet. I can do this. I must stay strong.' I sniffle while staring at the flickering flames. I miss my bed and heated house, the cozy blankets and delicious food, but if going back there means being forced back into that unbearable position, I'll take the forest anytime. It may seem like some temper tantrum, but to me, it is important that I get my point across. I'm not a show pony. I don't want every part of my life being dictated or to be driven down a path that I have no desire to cross. I haven't felt like myself for a long time. I had to escape, even if it's only for a little while. It was for my own sanity.

"Why are you crying, Y/N?" I gave a short scream and jumped after hearing the Owl King's voice from the mouth of the cave and swiftly turned to find his head peering into my temporary home from the top, masked and hanging upside-down. His hair was sopping wet and dripping with water, though he did not seem bothered by the heavy rain. With a sigh of relief, I shake my head at him with a slight smile. It was good to see him again, but he gave me quite a scare.

"Jesus, you have to stop popping up like that." Sniffling, I wipe my eyes as he responded.

"Sorry, force of habit." The owl man jumps down from the roof and enters the cave, revealing the dead rabbit in his hand held by the ears. My eyes drift down to it as he approached. "One must be silent if they wish to catch their prey."

"Am I prey to you?" I jokingly ask. Owen chuckles and settles down beside me before removing the mask from his face.

"No, but now that you mention it, you do look rather tasty." I narrow my eyes, not very appreciative of his comment, which makes him smile wider. "Just kidding." He then lifts the rabbit for me to see, waving its body a bit. "You've been looking a little sickly, I noticed, so I thought I'd catch you something. You do not detest rabbit as much as you do mice, do you?"

"At this point, I might even take the mouse, but yes, I think I can handle a rabbit better. It has more meat anyways." Delighted, the man smiles bigger.

"Would you like me to cook this for you? My stomach can handle raw meats, but I have cooked by means of fire before. I'm guessing, humans don't eat things as they are." I nod to confirm that.

"Eating raw meat can make me sick, so I'd appreciate it." I get up from my spot and walk over to where I keep my makeshift knives made out of stone and pick out the sharpest one, while Owen watches with a sharply tilted head. I had made plenty after the bear incident to have something protect myself if it or any other animal decides to wander in. Luckily, such a thing hasn't happened yet, but I feel safer having these readily available. Before returning to him, I also pick up a slab of wood that I found a couple days ago that I've carved to make a flat surface. It wasn't easy to do, but I think it'll make for a good cutting board. Hopefully, there won't be splinters in the meat when he uses it. Owen seemed lost when I placed these items in front of him, which I found a little funny. "These should help with skinning and gutting it," I explain, and his eyes seemed to light up in realization.

"Ah, right. You probably can't consume hair or bones either. You humans are strange things, aren't you?" He laughs as he places the rabbit on the wooden slab, while my nose scrunches up in disgust. Now that I think about it, I haven't seen him eat, and maybe that's a good thing, considering what he just told me.

"You mean you eat that too?"

"Well, yes. It saves me time. I just cough up all the indigestible stuff later." Fiddling with the knife, he attempts to cut into the animal a bit clumsily due to his nails. Perhaps it would've been easier for him to use the talons instead, but he looked too intrigued by the knife to stop using it. His words make me gag as I hide my mouth behind my hand. Such an image was disturbing. Owen tilts his head at me when I do this, pausing.

"Is that repulsive?"

"A... A little, but you do you." I lower my hand to give him a crooked grin, not wanting him to feel self-conscious about the way he eats. He seemed unbothered and went back to skinning as I looked him over. He was in owl form but still wore his cloak over his wings. No doubt he's warm under all those feathers; meanwhile, I'd kill for even a thin blanket at the moment. I raise my hands to my arms and scoot a bit closer to the flames while rubbing them. This did not go unnoticed by Owen's unusually large eyes. Humming, he sets down the stone to free up a hand before removing his cloak and holding it out to me.

"Take it."

"You sure?" I question while reaching out for the damp feathers. He nods, and so, I accept the cloak before he returns to preparing dinner. I don't hesitate to wrap myself up and am grateful for its thickness. The droplets of rain that coated the outer feathers didn't even touch the inside, which is soft and cozy. I shiver one last time as the warmth settled in before closing my eyes.

When I opened them again, I witnessed Owen cutting out organs and scrunched my nose as the animal was emptied. I thought it looked disgusting, but food is food, and I could really use some protein after having been chewing on fruit and whatever edible plants and mushrooms I could find. I only ate what I was certain wouldn't poison me. I'm glad I had that knowledge on hand, since it certainly came in handy for this situation. Even so, it hasn't felt like enough for me.

I suppose that's why Owen mentioned I looked a bit sickly. I could tell without even looking in a mirror that my body had changed from the lack of variety or even quantity for that matter. I hope to be able to catch something on my own soon, but I am very thankful to have Owen's help as well. I tried my hand at catching fish yesterday, but it's a lot harder than I thought it'd be. With some practice, I'm sure I'll be able to do it. Then, I won't have to rely on him to bring me food like this. "Thank you for this. It's been a while since I've had some decent food."

"I wouldn't want you starving under my watch. Besides, I think it'll be nice sharing a meal with you." His words warm my heart as I hold the cloak to my chin, cuddling into it as he stands up and wanders over to the collection of sharpened sticks I own. He picks out a short one before coming back to my side and secured the prepared rabbit by skewering it, then holds it over the fire to cook.

"You know, my dad used to tell me a story about you."

"About me?"

"I can't remember the exact story, but when I was little, he told me about an ancient forest where an owl king ruled. I wonder now if it was true, and if so, how he knew. I remember him telling me the story was passed down, however, so who knows?"

"Perhaps your ancestors had a run-in with mine in the past? It's not impossible. Though it's not often humans can wander into the forest, they could've met outside of it."

"Do you ever leave?"

"Sometimes, but not very often. I prefer it here. It's not as noisy as your cities. Most times when I do leave, it's only to check on human progress, which was something my family often did. They didn't want too many to discover this sacred place in fear that it'd fall to ruin, that the humans would only consume the land. I try to uphold that, since I too fear such an event."

"How come only some can see the entrance? I've had people tell me that I'm crazy because of it," I ask, having wondered that for a long time. They assumed I overworked myself into delusion and continually brushed it off.

"I can't quite explain it myself, but I'll try. The doorway, it's like a rift into another world. Sometimes it phases in and out— Weak in the perception of others, so it appears invisible to most. I'm not sure why they exist, just that I must watch them closely to keep anything bad from coming in or going out. That has been my family's purpose because our eyes can see all the portals. There are other creatures in this forest that are similar to me. Some are undesirable and dangerous, so it's important to guard these openings. There are more guards than myself, though there are few families anymore. Mine is the head, the ones in charge that gave orders to the other branches of families. That is the true reason of why I bear the title of king, though in truth, I believe I'd more resemble a... a... commander? General? I don't quite know the human terms for it. The leader is essentially what I'm getting at. It has been a long time since I've last heard from anyone, though," he claims with a gloomy voice, which made me feel sad.

He's been lonely, hasn't he? Nearly, I jumped at the crack of thunder outside, which boomed and echoed through the forest as lightning flashed through the sky. The winds shrieked with speeds that seemed to be ripping branches right off the trees. The combination of loud sounds made my heart race with fear that the storm might worsen throughout the night. I might not be able to sleep a wink. Owen removed the rabbit from the fire after it seemed done and stared off with a blank expression.

"The storm looks pretty bad. Do you maybe want to stay here with me tonight if the rain won't let up?" My suggestion broke him from his thoughts, and he looked towards me with a little smile.

"Are you afraid?" he questions with amusement, which makes me pout a little. I went to retort when thunder rumbled the earth. It made me tense.

"Not afraid, exactly, but it does make me nervous. There have been many rainstorms since I've been here, but this one seems pretty bad." Owen looked like he wanted to say something, but shut his mouth a moment later and said something else instead.

"It will end soon, I'm sure, but I will stay if you want me to." He split open the rabbit to rip off a portion before giving it to me. "Here, it should be cooled enough now."

"Thank you." I blow on it just to be sure and check if it was cooked all the way before taking a hesitant bite. There were no spices to flavor it, but it did kind of taste like chicken, so it wasn't bad. My hungry stomach couldn't care less anyways. It was the best thing I've eaten since I left home. Owen takes off the whole back leg for himself before opening his mouth wide. It was in partway when I noticed. The man didn't even choke. Catching my stare, he stopped and pulled the leg out with some embarrassment.

"Pardon me. I'll refrain from eating that way in your presence." I shake my head, realizing the look I must've made and wave my hand around.

"Sorry, it's just a little weird to me." I look away, shifting my gaze over to the plush, rabbit fur that was discarded on the ground. Owen managed to get it off in practically one piece, and it was a decent-sized rabbit. I'll be sure to make use of it later, perhaps to rest my head upon at night while I sleep so that I'm not lying directly on the dirt, but I'll have to wash it in the stream first.

"I find some of the things you do strange as well, so I understand," he claims while looking over the stone knife he used earlier before biting into the rabbit leg normally. I move in closer to him and notice him tensing up a bit, probably because he didn't know my intentions.

"I realize that. You seem nervous of me sometimes, and I don't blame you, really. It's as you said, humans don't exactly have the best reputation."

"You are not as bad as I expected you to be, Y/N," he assures, which makes me smile.

"Same goes for you. I thought you were pretty scary, but you're actually really nice. I like you. I like this forest too. It's beautiful here, and I'm glad it has someone like you protecting it. I've experienced so many things I never got to before. I had never seen so many beautiful sights, never got to step foot in a natural hot spring before, let alone bathe in one. I've never met a creature like you or got a chance to touch the clouds. I've never felt more free than I do here."

I laugh softly and wipe a few tears that had gathered in my eyes as Owen watched me fondly. I give a shaky breath before meeting his orange gaze with a sad smile on my lips. "But, unfortunately, I will have to go back one day, and I hate knowing that with each day that passes, the closer I'll be to that time. I want to stay as long as I can because I know that once I go back home, I might never get this freedom again." I look down again at the fire, holding back the urge to cry, and sniffle. I can play survivalist all I like, but I know I'm not capable of staying here forever.

"That is because of your mother, right?" I nod.

"She just keeps pushing me. I hardly ever have the time to do the things I like or have fun because of her." I didn't bother to bring up all the school clubs I was forced to go to since a young age, all the advanced classes and studying, knowing that he might have no clue what I'm talking about. "Even the 'friends' I have were practically picked out by her, and without question, they'd all leave me in a heartbeat. They all think I'm some workaholic and talk bad about me behind my back, but I put up with it because my mom says their parents are successful, which apparently, will lead to great connections for the future." I scoff. "She's so controlling over every aspect of my life even though I'm clearly suffering because of it. I don't have a choice in anything."

"Have you told her this?" I nod my head again.

"Many times, but she says it's only a phase and that I'll understand when I'm older." Dropping the, now bare, bones, I raise a hand to my forehead and take a few deep breaths. Owen looks me over in concern with a deep frown on his face. He could see me struggling to keep it together. I feel like I'm about to burst.

"I had to run away. I had to be on my own someplace I wouldn't have to hear her nagging voice pointing out every little flaw. I just wanted peace. All I want is peace." A sob catches in my throat as my left hand joins the other in covering my face. I continue biting back tears, though some managed to slip by regardless.

I hear a trill amongst the thunder before feeling a nudge against the side of my head. I lower my arms and look over at Owen, who continues nestling against me. With an outstretched wing, he wraps me up and brings me close, which releases the rest of my tears. With a gentle claw, he held my face and pressed his forehead to mine as I pulled the cloak in closer. His eyes stared in pity, and I could not look at them for long. I thought this "adventure" was something to be ashamed of, that everyone around me would think I was being stupid. To finally be seen by another person was liberating.

"You are always welcome here. You may find your peace in this forest anytime you wish. No matter the day, month or year. If you need an escape, I promise, you have a place here." When he lifted his head, I looked up with crying eyes.

"C- Can I hug you?" Tilting his head a bit, Owen shifted himself and set down the remains of the rabbit before slipping his claws around my back. The sharp points of his talons made me flinch but did not detour me from wrapping my arms around his neck and burying my face against his feathery chest. I took to sobbing as the storm outside began to let up to a gentle drizzle. I hardly noticed the sudden change in weather as I whimpered and cried.

All I could focus on were his comforting hands and the wings that cocooned around me.

— — — — — — — — — — — — — — — —
_____Author's
Note:_____

Hope you enjoyed the chapter, everyone!

I just wanted you to tell you all some important news, so please, continue reading this note for me while I explain. I started a Quotev account some time ago, since Wattpad was deleting some of my books, so if you've been looking for them, that's where they are posted. Keep in mind that the account is still new, so I haven't been able to post everything yet, but I plan to put all the books I have here as well. Now, I don't expect Wattpad to delete any more of my books, but if they do or if they do something else to upset me, I more then likely will be deleting this account entirely and moving to Quotev completely, which is why it's so important that you follow me there.

This is a worst-case scenario. As I said, I don't expect them to screw me over again, but I've given them too many chances already. I'm trying to reach as many of you as possible so that you're all informed in case I decide to, you know, drop off the face of the earth. Anyways, the account is under the same username: Goldenscares666

And, if you need the link, here's that too:

https://www.quotev.com/Goldenscares666

Again, this is just a precaution. Still, I'd really appreciate it if you followed me there.

Thank you for reading,

~Golden~

Journey of Independence

● Y/N: Your Name

——————————————————————————Author's

POV:_____

_____

The chirping of warblers acted as a morning alarm and broke Y/N out of her dreams that fled from memory the moment her sleepy eyes opened. With a yawn, she sat up, her back not feeling as sore as she was used to due to the cushioning of Owen's cloak which had been wrapped around her form throughout the night. When she looked around for the birdlike man, however, she found him missing from the cave which had disappointed her just slightly. Y/N lingers in her resting spot, recalling last night how the Owl King had held and comforted her. She had never broken down like that in front of anybody before, so naturally, she felt a little embarrassed about how she behaved.

Perhaps, it was a good thing he was not there when she woke? At least, that's what she assumed. Had she peeked outside and up at the nearest tree, she would've found him there, watching with keen eyes, mask on his face and surrounded by a few small owls. They slept on the branches around him, while he remained awake, also reminiscing the night. Y/N had fallen asleep not long after they had finished the rabbit, guts and all, leaving nothing but bones and fur.

He felt pity for the poor creature. She held so much pain that she had attempted to hide for as long as she could hold out but, in the end, confessed all that brought her misery. He saw now why she felt like she had to run away. He had felt freedom all his life and could not possibly imagine such a thing. Groaning, the girl gets to her feet and dusts off before bending down to pick up the male's cloak. She folds it neatly before setting it down and grabbing a small stone to mark the wall.

She was coming on eleven days now, and after confiding in Owen, she felt more confident than ever about staying as long as possible. She wasn't going to cave in, and she wasn't going to let nature get the better of her. It's time to wise up and learn how to hunt her own food, and that's exactly what she wants to accomplish today. She would even settle on a newt or frog if she must. With a smile on her lips, Y/N steps outside of the cave momentarily and looks down at the collection of rocks she had set out yesterday and find all the divots filled with fresh rainwater from the storm last night.

It may not be the best method for catching water, but it was helpful nonetheless. She couldn't exactly fashion a proper bowl or jug with the materials she has. One by one, they're carefully brought inside and set down, save for one, which she takes a sip out of to hydrate. Before stepping away to her stash of fruit, which are kept wrapped up in her white scarf in a hidden crevice. She picks a few berries out of her rations and pops them into her mouth. As she eats, the young woman wonders if she should wait for Owen to return or if he'd even be returning to the cave today. Surely, he would have to retrieve his cloak, right? As the thought crossed her mind, Y/N looked down at the feathery cloak.

'I might as well wear it while he's away. If he wants it back, he could easily find me.' Glad to have the extra warmth on hand, she dons the heavy piece of clothing, which weighs down on her shoulders, before picking up what she might need for today: two stone knives and a sharpened stick. She reminds herself to stick to the hunting rules set by the owl-man — not to kill something that would disrupt the balance — and decides to give fishing another shot. So, she sets out, armed and ready for the new day, and gazes up at the sky to find it partially cloudy.

This was pretty good, considering the usual, dreary mornings. Following close behind like a shadow was her watcher who moved through the branches of trees fluidly. She payed no mind to the rustling leaves as she trudged through mud and bugs, scratching at a mosquito bite or two that she had gotten the night prior. She wished she had something to relieve the annoying itch but had no choice but to wait for them to heal on their own. Once at the stream, she unloaded her things before waiting by the bank on top of a fallen tree with her wooden spear in hand.

Many branches had fallen due to the storm, and it seemed not even the trees were spared. She waited there a while before moving further down the log, which stuck out over a portion of the water. Again, she sat for about half an hour and could feel the sun beating on her skin as it shone through the clouds. She was sure to cover up using the cloak, but all she could do to protect her face was to turn away from the sun.

Some fish swam by, albeit small ones that were hardly worth catching, and she was starting to lose hope when a group of rainbow trout appeared below. Gasping, she readied herself, but was careful not to move too suddenly, as not to scare the fish. She carefully watched them swim and took in account the refraction of light before striking. The first was a miss and sent the creatures away, but she quickly took a second shot before they were out of reach, and to her utter disbelief, she had caught one. It flopped frantically on the spear and nearly slipped off, but she swiftly pulled it near and gripped its tail tight before moving back to land where she then jumped around and danced in victory, laughing with excitement.

"I did it! I did it! I actually caught a fish!" she shouted, making Owen laugh softly from his spot in the tree as he drew his knees to his chest. He watched her fondly as he folded up his arms and rested his chin on them. His eyelids drooped tiredly, but he could not stop watching her. He simply couldn't bring himself to look away, yet he couldn't figure out the reason why. Feeling confident now, Y/N removed her boots and socks before rolling up her pants to enter the water for more. Meanwhile, a small, black owl perches on a branch slightly above Owen's head and hoots before bending down to tug at a strand of his brown hair. Attention diverted, he smiles at the bird and pets its head with a gentle finger before looking back at the human as she eagerly waited for more fish.

"She's quite silly, don't you think?" He asks the owl with a smile on his lips. The animal coos, and he nods his head in agreement, having understood what they had said.

"Yes, that too. It'll be lonely when she leaves." At that, he sighed, and the sun was once again covered by fluffy, white clouds that cast a shadow over the forest below. The owl hoots again, causing his head to perk as his eyes widen. He faces the bird with a scolding stare.

"No, I couldn't! What a terrible suggestion. 'Keep her here'. That wouldn't be right." Huffing, Owen peers back down at the girl who catches yet another fish.

"Hell yeah! I'm eating good tonight!" Her comment brings back out a proud smile as he mutters more words.

"Besides, this is her journey to prove herself. I can't be selfish. Perhaps she'll visit me? That'd be nice." With a final hoot, the small owl flies off, and the man heaves a sigh before leaning back and stretching out his long legs along the branch.

'It's truly a shame that Y/N can't stay,' he thought. Owen found enjoyment in her company, but she was not so apt at living in the wilderness as he. She would reach her limit eventually, but he would ensure she could hold out for a good while. He didn't want her to go back to feeling miserable. It is a horrid feeling to have.

He wants her to succeed, but at the same time, he also doesn't want to baby her. She's obviously knowledgeable about her surroundings, so he didn't want her to feel like the only reason she was doing so well was because of his help. That absolutely wasn't the case. He gave her assistance, sure, but she would've eventually had a handle on things with a little more exploration, even if he wasn't present. Really, the only thing he did that he thought was noteworthy was setting up protection around her camp; although, she seemed to like his company as well. With a light trill, his claws tightened on the branch as his chest warmed. By midday, Y/N called it quits and brought her kill back to the cave with a pep in her step, but Owen remained by the stream and closed his eyes with a content sigh.

"I hope you stay for a long time, Y/N. I have been lonely for too long."

CPSIA information can be obtained
at www.ICGtesting.com
Printed in the USA
BVHW070528140123
656277BV00014B/1244